MEDIEVAL KNIGHTS

by Molly Jones

Published by The Child's World
1980 Lookout Drive • Mankato, MN 56003-1705
800-599-READ • www.childsworld.com

ACKNOWLEDGMENTS
The Child's World: Mary Berendes, Publishing Director
Red Line Editorial: Editorial direction
The Design Lab: Design
Amnet: Production
Content Consultant: Theresa Gross-Diaz, Associate Professor
of History, Loyola University Chicago
Design elements: iStockphoto
Photographs ©: Bettmann/Corbis/AP Images, cover; Gianni
Dagli Orti/Corbis, 4; Tarker/Corbis, 6, 30 (bottom left);
Chris Hellier/Corbis, 8; Marzolino/Shutterstock Images, 11,
30 (top); Stapleton Collection/Corbis, 12; Purestock/Think-
stock Images, 13; Mike Kemp/Rubberball/Corbis, 16; Tibor
Bognar/Corbis, 17, 30 (bottom right); Bettmann/Corbis,
19, 23; adoc-photos/Corbis, 20; Alfredo Dagli Orti/The Art
Archive/Corbis, 22; Dorling Kindersley/Thinkstock Images,
24; The Gallery Collection/Corbis, 27

ISBN 9781631437557
LCCN 2014945425

Printed in the United States of America
Mankato, MN
November, 2014
PA02246

ABOUT THE AUTHOR

Molly Jones lives on Lake Murray in the midlands of South Carolina. She likes to sail, practice yoga, and write books for young readers. Her previous books have covered history, controversial issues, and health development topics.

TABLE OF CONTENTS

Knights looked powerful dressed in their armor riding into battle.

CHAPTER ONE

A BRAVE YOUNG KNIGHT OF ARAGON

A thousand years ago in Europe, a knight was the hero of his village. Ordinary soldiers marched on foot, but crowds gathered to watch a knight ride by on his horse. Both knights and foot soldiers were important parts of an army.

One young knight and king was James I. In 1208, James I was born to King Peter II and his wife, Mary. King Peter II ruled a large part of Spain called Aragon. As king, he also led the knights of his kingdom. He and his knights were always ready to defend their kingdom from its enemies. As the king's

Medieval armies used hurling machines to attack walled cities.

In one night, the hurling machine threw 500 stones. In one full day, it threw 1,000 more.

By evening, the stones broke through the castle wall. The army marched in and freed the knight. James I, the young king and knight, had led his soldiers to victory.

Hurling Machines

A fonevol and trebuchet were two kinds of hurling machines. Hurling machines could throw large stones to damage castle walls. They could throw dead animals over the walls. The animals spread disease and odor inside the castle grounds. The attackers sometimes threw the heads of enemy soldiers. They hoped the heads would frighten the people inside into surrendering.

Another View
Child Rulers

James I became king of Aragon at age six. At ten, he led knights in battle. He was married at age 13. In the 12th century, Baldwin IV became king of Jerusalem at age 13. In the United States, children at those ages cannot yet vote. How do you think young rulers felt about having so many responsibilities?

CHAPTER TWO

THE ORIGINS OF KNIGHTHOOD

The Middle Ages lasted approximately from the years 500 to 1500. During this time, Europe was made up of many kingdoms. Around the year 771, King Charlemagne ruled the Frankish kingdom. His territory included much of present-day France, Belgium, Luxembourg, the Netherlands, and western Germany. By the early ninth century, he ruled most of Western Europe. In 800, the religious leader Pope Leo III crowned Charlemagne emperor.

Charlemagne's armies helped him expand and defend his large kingdom. They also helped him govern his people and manage his land.

Before this, armies in Europe had been mostly foot soldiers, or **infantry**. Gradually, mounted warriors

King Charlemagne was a powerful ruler during the Middle Ages.

replaced many of the foot soldiers. These soldiers rode on horseback and were called **cavalry**. They could carry heavy weapons and armor. They could also ride to and from battle sites quickly. Though knights usually rode on horses, they occasionally fought on foot.

However, not everyone could join the cavalry. Only wealthy soldiers could afford horses as well as weapons and armor. Charlemagne rewarded the **nobles** who served in the cavalry. He granted them parcels of his land called **fiefs**. Some soldiers who received fiefs became lords and were called knights. In return, they could award parcels of their land to other lords and knights.

A knight protected his castle and land.

Some knights lived in manors, or castles. They governed and defended their land. Many knights did not own land. They served and protected a lord's land and castle.

At the end of the 11th century, knights also defended the Christian Church. They served both the pope and the emperor. As soldiers, they were sometimes sent to war in enemy lands.

Peasants worked as craftsmen, shopkeepers, or farmers. They also served as soldiers when needed.

A Templar knight kneels during his knighting ceremony.

Most peasants did not own their own land. They lived on the fief of a lord.

An order was a group of knights who shared the same code of behavior and goals. The first order was the Hospitallers, started in 1113. These knights cared for sick or wounded **pilgrims**. The Knights Templar was another order, which started in 1118. They protected Christian pilgrims traveling to Jerusalem. Other orders were established between the 12th and 15th centuries.

The Code of Chivalry

Knights were skilled in war. But they also vowed to obey a code of behavior. This code was known as **chivalry**. A knight vowed to defend the helpless, especially women and children. He also vowed to be religious, honest, courteous, **chaste**, and loyal.

Another View
Infantry or Cavalry

A cavalry soldier rode on horseback in battle. His travel was less tiring and faster than traveling on foot. Often, the horse's hooves acted as weapons. However, foot soldiers only had to worry about their own safety, not the safety of a horse. Losing a fine horse in battle was costly. How do you think cavalry and infantry soldiers felt about using horses in battle?

CHAPTER THREE

WEAPONS AND ARMOR

Almost every knight carried a sword. The sword could be used as either a slashing or thrusting weapon. The knight's sword was a symbol of his loyalty to his vows of chivalry. Often, a priest blessed the sword in a special ceremony. Sometimes, the knight named his sword and treated it as a sacred friend.

Most knights wore mail armor in battles. A blacksmith made mail from thin sheets of metal. First, he made the sheets into wires or narrow strips. Next, he made these into small circles and linked them into chains or clusters. Finally, he linked the chains or clusters to create a flexible metal fabric. Mail was light to wear but very strong.

A knight wore mail on his body where he was most likely to get hurt in battle. A mail shirt covered the knight's chest, abdomen, arms, and back. Mail stockings covered his legs. A mail hood protected his head. Cloth garments worn under mail protected a knight's skin from the metal. A helmet and jacket or coat added protection over the mail.

A knight's sword and shield were important battle tools.

A club or the long edge of a sword could not easily pierce mail. But sharp, fast arrows did pierce mail. The point of a sword or spear could also pierce mail. Metal plates of armor began to replace or cover mail in the 13th century. These plates provided greater protection for the warriors.

Plate armor was made in several pieces. Each piece covered a different body area. The plates were connected with movable rivets and leather straps. These allowed the knight to move freely while wearing the separate plates. An entire suit of battle armor usually weighed between 45 and 55 pounds (20 and 25 kg). The knight's helmet weighed between 4 and 8 pounds (2 and 4 kg). A knight's horse wore mail or plate armor, too. The armor covered its head, neck, body, and chest. Padded cloth covered the horse's rear to cushion its flesh.

Armor protected both a knight and his horse from harm.

A knight's spear could reach farther than his sword. But to fight across longer distances, armies depended on archers. The archers fought beside the knights and infantry. Their arrows protected the knights and foot soldiers. The distance arrows could fly depended on the type of bow and the skill of the archer. Longbow arrows could fly from short distances up to several hundred yards.

Sometimes archers shot burning arrows across fields or over walls.

Siege weapons helped an attacking army break through castle walls. The knights and soldiers could then enter and capture the people inside. By the 12th century, hurling machines were important in sieges. As castle walls were built stronger and higher, stronger hurling machines were developed. These machines could throw heavier objects higher and farther than before.

To knock down a door or wall, some armies used a battering ram. This was a large tree trunk or pole. The ram was hung from ropes and rolled on a cart. Once in place against a wall, the attackers swung it back and forth. The repeated blows eventually broke through thick doors and walls.

Late in the 14th century, a major development changed battle tactics used by armies. Gunpowder was used for the first time on the medieval battlefield. Soon guns and cannons were developed. Their range and power made earlier medieval weapons less useful. Since infantry operated most firing weapons, knights became less important in battle.

Medieval armies used different siege weapons to crash through castle walls.

The Knight's Helper

A **squire** was a knight in training. Often, he had been training for knighthood from a young age. Before becoming a squire, he served as a page in the knight's castle. When he was older, he learned knighthood skills by helping the knight he served. The squire helped his knight dress for battle. He also took care of the knight's armor, weapons, and horse. When the knight believed the squire was ready, the squire became a knight, too.

ANOTHER VIEW

SQUIRES AND KNIGHTS

Knights were dependent on their squires. The success of the squire depended on learning from the knight. If you were a squire, how would you feel when your knight won in battle?

A squire (left) helps a Templar knight with his horse.

CHAPTER FOUR

BATTLE TACTICS

In battles, knights and foot soldiers fought within reach of the enemy. They battled one on one. But in medieval times, there were more sieges than battles as knights fought to gain land.

To gain control of a territory, knights had to conquer each fief. Sometimes the knight acquired a fief by marriage. He or a member of his family might marry a person in a lord's family. Other times, a lord might surrender a fief to avoid a conflict. Otherwise, the castle had to be taken by force. Often the knight ordered a siege to capture the castle.

In a siege, the attackers first surrounded the castle. No one was allowed to enter or leave it. The attackers

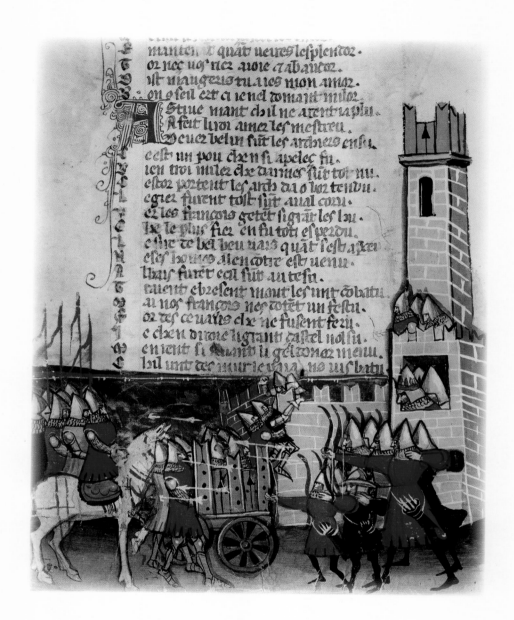

A medieval manuscript shows knights
surrounding a castle during a siege.

hoped to starve those inside and cause them to give up. If this failed, the attackers broke into the castle. Once inside, the knights and their army took everyone prisoner.

Armies often used a siege tower to break into a castle. The wooden tower was built on top of a rolling platform. The tower was rolled to the wall. Then a hurling machine

Knights could attack the top of a castle wall in a siege tower.

THE JOUST

The joust was a contest between two knights. Armed with swords or lances, the knights fought a mock battle. By jousting, knights displayed their courage and skill. Jousting also helped them maintain and sharpen their skills. A system of points decided the winner. Most jousts were friendly games. However, some resulted in serious injuries or deaths.

Knights used lances to joust at a medieval contest.

or battering ram could be mounted on the tower. From the upper part of the tower, objects were thrown over the castle wall. From the lower part, the attacking army might dig under the wall. To further the attack, knights might order their army to poison the castle well. They sometimes burned crops, too.

Behind the wall, defenders might build a tower as well. From the top, they could hurl stones or arrows on the attackers. Either side might try to knock over or set fire to the other's tower.

Another View
The Dark Side of Knighthood

At times knights displayed chivalry only toward other nobility. To servants and others, knights were sometimes rude or even brutal. They often allowed their armies to kill their captives. When fighting in another country, knights might rob, murder, or burn the crops of people who tried to help them. Their victims were often helpless to defend themselves. How do you think peasants felt about medieval knights who treated them poorly?

CHAPTER FIVE

KNIGHTS IN BATTLE

In 1066, there was a fight for the throne of England. William of Normandy was a duke from northern France. The previous English king, Edward, had promised the throne to Duke William. But as he was dying, King Edward changed his mind. He named Harold II the new English king. Duke William was not willing to give in though. Neither was King Harold II.

To settle the matter, Duke William brought 7,000 troops including knights and their horses on boats from France. They landed in Hastings, a town in southern England. Soon, King Harold II arrived. Leading his army, he was prepared to defend his throne.

On October 14, the armies met in a fierce battle. The well-trained infantry of King Harold II waited

The Bayeux Tapestry depicts Duke William and his knights on horseback as they battled the English.

on a ridge for the army's attack. Duke William's army contained both foot soldiers and many knights on horseback. At times it seemed that the English had won. But after hours of battle, Duke William's army caught the English off guard. His cavalry charged the English troops and victory was his. William the Conqueror, as he became known, was soon crowned the king of England.

In Italy, a different kind of war was brewing. In 1095, Pope Urban II made a grave speech. The Turkish army, whose religion was Islam, had captured the Holy

City of Jerusalem. He called on Christians to fight to take it back. This was the start of the First Crusade.

Knights in Europe had vowed to defend the Christian Church. Also, the pope promised great spiritual rewards for those who answered his call. Thousands of knights agreed to march to Jerusalem. Then, surprisingly, thousands more joined them. The knights along with peasants, children, and entire families began their journeys to Jerusalem.

Many crusaders died from thirst, exhaustion, and injuries on the way. After a seven-month battle, they finally captured the Turkish city of Antioch. Finally, in 1099, the crusaders captured Jerusalem. The crusaders killed almost the entire population of Jerusalem.

Christian and Turkish armies continued to battle over Jerusalem. In 1291, after eight Crusades, the Turks finally won.

By the 14th and early 15th centuries, battle weapons had changed. For hundreds of years, knights had enjoyed great honor and privilege. As modern life and technology replaced medieval ways, knights became a part of history.

Knighthood Today

Modern knights no longer fight in battles. Instead, knighthood, or damehood for women, is a special honor. In the United Kingdom, the king or queen awards knighthood to outstanding individuals. These people have made major contributions to the country in fields such as the arts or national service. Musician Paul McCartney and Prime Minister Winston Churchill both received this honor.

Another View
FEMALE KNIGHTS

While a few women became knights, they rarely bore the military responsibilities of males. Occasionally, a medieval woman became a knight when given a fief. Some women became knights when admitted into an order of knights. The Order of the Hatchet was founded in 1149 in Spain. The order rewarded women who had fought to defend their towns. In Italy in 1233, the Order of the Glorious Saint Mary was created. This was the first religious order to grant knighthood to women. How do you think medieval women felt about becoming knights?

TIMELINE

500
The Middle Ages begins around this time.

800
Pope Leo III crowns Charlemagne the emperor.

1066
The Battle of Hastings occurs.

1118
The order of the Knights Templar forms.

1208
James I of Aragon is born.

1291
The Turks capture Jerusalem after eight Crusades.

Late 14th century
Gunpowder is first used on the medieval battlefield.

1500
The Middle Ages comes to an end around this time.

GLOSSARY

cavalry (KAV-uhl-ree) Cavalry are soldiers who ride on horseback. Knights were part of the cavalry.

chaste (CHAYST) To be chaste is to be morally pure and decent. To obey the code of chivalry, knights promised to be chaste.

chivalry (SHIV-uhl-ree) Chivalry is a code of noble and polite behavior. Knights promised to follow a code of chivalry.

fiefs (FEEFS) Fiefs are estates of land owned by lords. Knights were given fiefs by the king.

infantry (IN-fuhn-tree) An infantry is a group of soldiers who fight on foot. Infantry soldiers fought beside knights in battle.

medieval (mee-DEE-vuhl) Something that is medieval comes from the time of the Middle Ages. In medieval wars, knights wore armor to protect their bodies from harm.

nobles (NOH-buhlz) Nobles are people from important or ruling families. Kings granted knighthood to nobles.

peasants (PEZ-uhnts) During Medieval times, peasants were people who worked on small farms or did other labor. Most peasants did not own land.

pilgrims (PIL-gruhmz) Pilgrims are people who travel to a holy place where they can worship. Knights protected pilgrims as they traveled to Jerusalem.

siege (SEEJ) A siege is when troops surround a city or other area to cause its people to surrender. Knights and infantry laid siege to castles during the Middle Ages.

squire (SKWIRE) A squire was a nobleman who traveled with and helped a knight. A squire trained to become a knight.

TO LEARN MORE

BOOKS

Dixon, Phillip. *Knights and Castles*.
New York: Simon and Schuster, 2008.

Walker, Jane. *Knights and Castles*. New York:
Gareth Stevens Publishing, 2015.

WEB SITES

Visit our Web site for links about medieval knights:

childsworld.com/links

Note to Parents, Teachers, and Librarians: We routinely verify our Web links to make sure they are safe and active sites. So encourage your readers to check them out!

INDEX